COLLEGE · CHILDREN'S · LITERATURE · FESTIVAL · THE · KEENE · STATE

TRAVELS
FOR TWO

Stories and lies from my childhood

TRAVELS FOR TWO

Stories and lies from my childhood

Stéphane Poulin
Annick Press

Designed by
Stéphane Poulin
Graphic Design by
Catherine Bouchard
Typography
Mimotype

Annick Press gratefully
acknowledges the support
of The Canada Council and
The Ontario Arts Council

**Canadian Cataloguing in
Publication Data**

Poulin, Stéphane
    [Voyage pour deux.
    English]
    Travels for two

(Stories and lies from my
childhood)
Issued also in French under
title: **Un voyage pour deux.**
ISBN 1-55037-20-5-X (bound)
ISBN 1-55037-204-1 (pbk.)

I. Title. II. Title: Voyage pour
deux. English. III. Series:
Poulin, Stéphane. Stories
and lies from my childhood.

PS8581.065V613   1991
jC843'.54
C91-094420-2
PZ7.P68Tr   1991

Distributed in Canada
and the USA by:
Firefly Books Ltd.
250 Sparks Avenue
Willowdale, Ontario, Canada
M2H 2S4

♾ This book is printed on
acid free paper.

Printed and bound in Canada
by D.W. Friesen & Sons, Ltd.

To Félix,
Monique and Louis.

When I was young, I lived in the country, between two cabbage fields, in a little house that was almost as small as I was. My family lived a quiet, peaceful life. Nothing ever happened to us.

Nothing that is, until the day the postman brought my mother a letter that changed all that. My mother looked at it and then, her voice trembling, read it aloud.

Dear Madam,
    It is with great pleasure that we inform you that you are the lucky **winner** of a **magnificent** trip for two to cruise the **tropics**. . .

We were all leaping and dancing with joy when my mother suddenly stopped and re-read the letter... *"a magnificent trip for two..."*

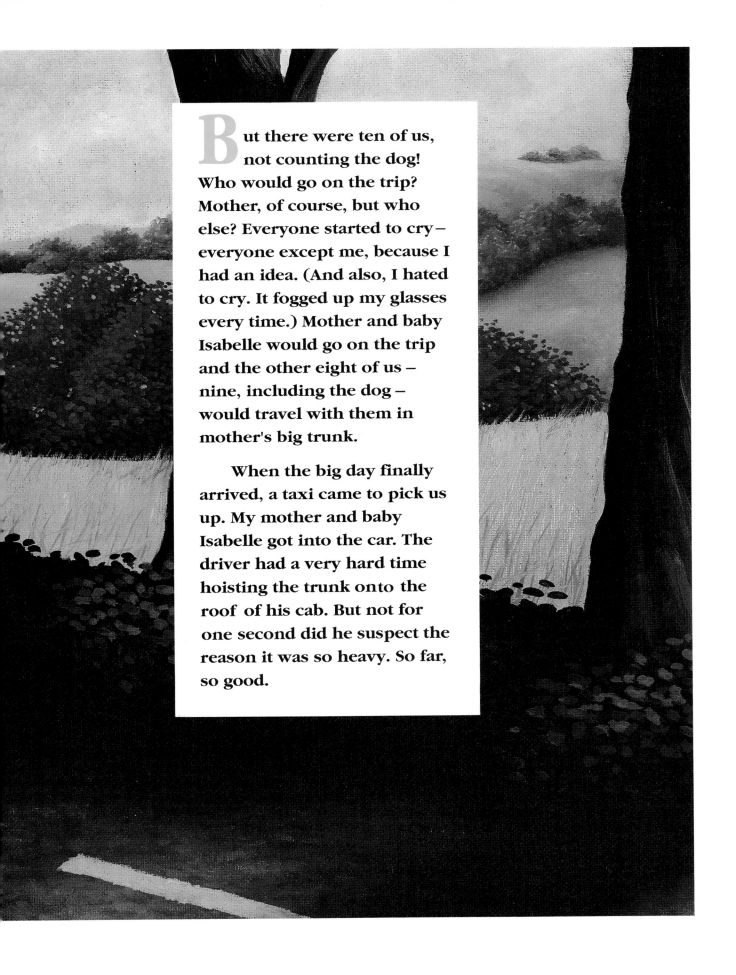

But there were ten of us, not counting the dog! Who would go on the trip? Mother, of course, but who else? Everyone started to cry — everyone except me, because I had an idea. (And also, I hated to cry. It fogged up my glasses every time.) Mother and baby Isabelle would go on the trip and the other eight of us — nine, including the dog — would travel with them in mother's big trunk.

When the big day finally arrived, a taxi came to pick us up. My mother and baby Isabelle got into the car. The driver had a very hard time hoisting the trunk onto the roof of his cab. But not for one second did he suspect the reason it was so heavy. So far, so good.

My mother and Isabelle boarded the airplane that would take us to the cruise ship. But no sooner had we taken off than our plan started to fall apart. The dog had to go to the bathroom; then Martine, Normand and Johanne had to go, too. Wait a minute – we all decided we had to go. Panic! Real Panic! When the flight attendant saw us coming she screamed. The passengers were outraged, the dog started to bark, and baby Isabelle bawled.

My brothers and sisters were running around everywhere. The pilot was furious and told us to leave. Leave? No way! We quickly hid in the trunk. My mother and Isabelle climbed in with us.

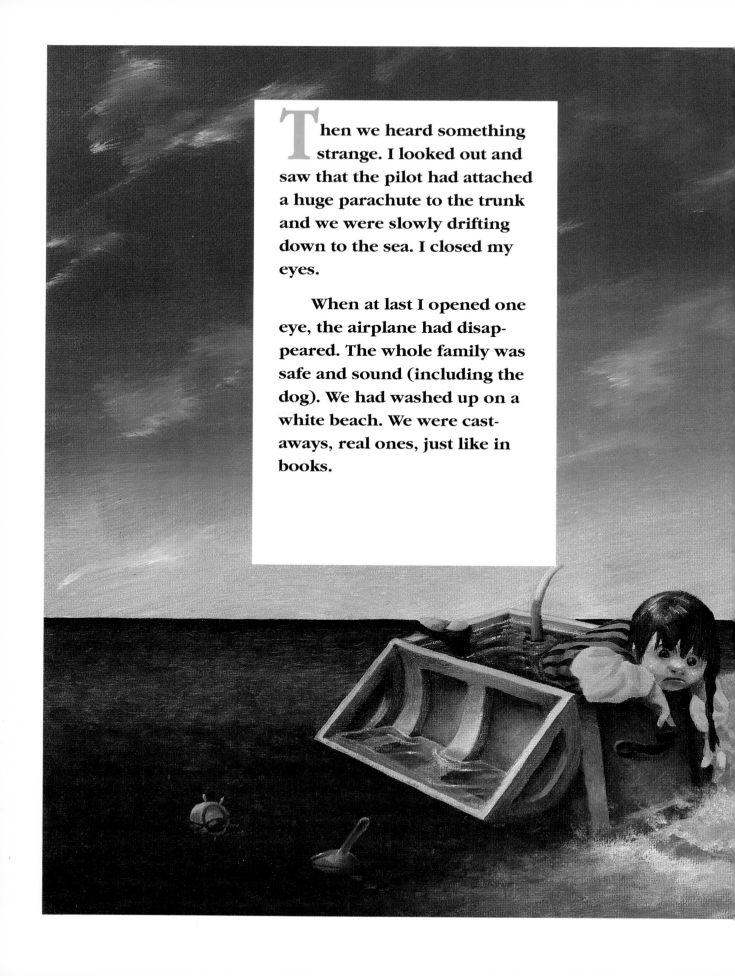

Then we heard something
strange. I looked out and
saw that the pilot had attached
a huge parachute to the trunk
and we were slowly drifting
down to the sea. I closed my
eyes.

When at last I opened one
eye, the airplane had disap-
peared. The whole family was
safe and sound (including the
dog). We had washed up on a
white beach. We were cast-
aways, real ones, just like in
books.

We soon discovered that we were marooned on an island. A deserted island.

The days went by. This was the ideal place for a holiday: sea, beaches, warm sand, caves to hide in, delicious tropical fruits... This was bliss.

We wanted this dream life to last forever. But one morning a ship dropped anchor near our beach.

At first we thought someone had come to rescue us. But, oh no, they were pirates. Frightened, we ran to hide in the sand dunes.

We heard the captain yelling at his men. They had come to get a treasure chest that had been buried on the island years ago.

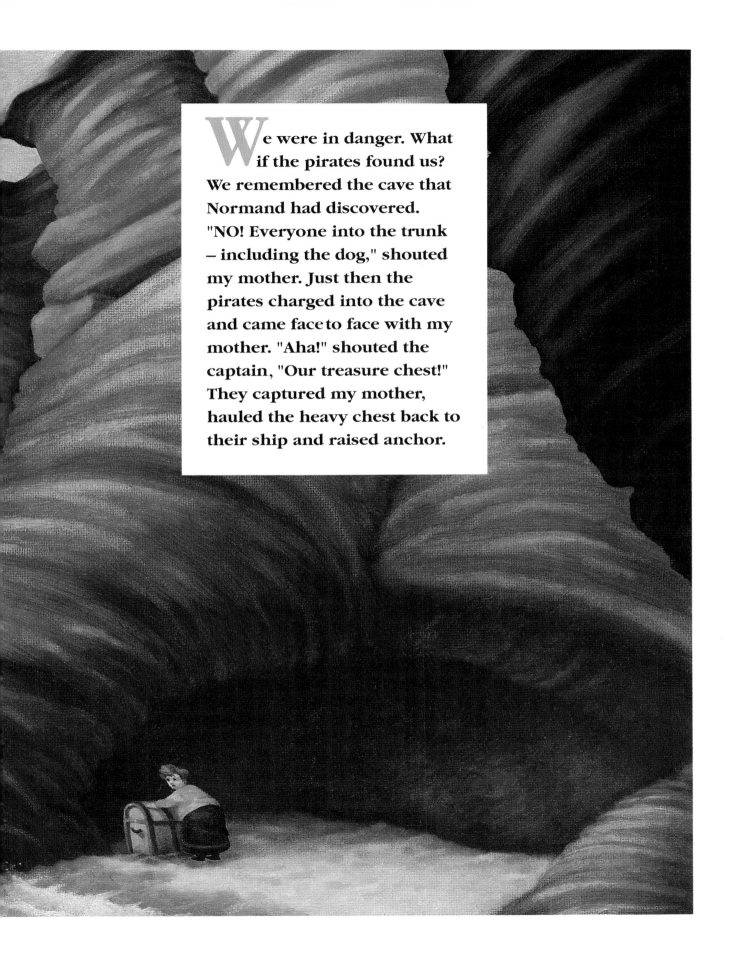

We were in danger. What if the pirates found us? We remembered the cave that Normand had discovered. "NO! Everyone into the trunk – including the dog," shouted my mother. Just then the pirates charged into the cave and came face to face with my mother. "Aha!" shouted the captain, "Our treasure chest!" They captured my mother, hauled the heavy chest back to their ship and raised anchor.

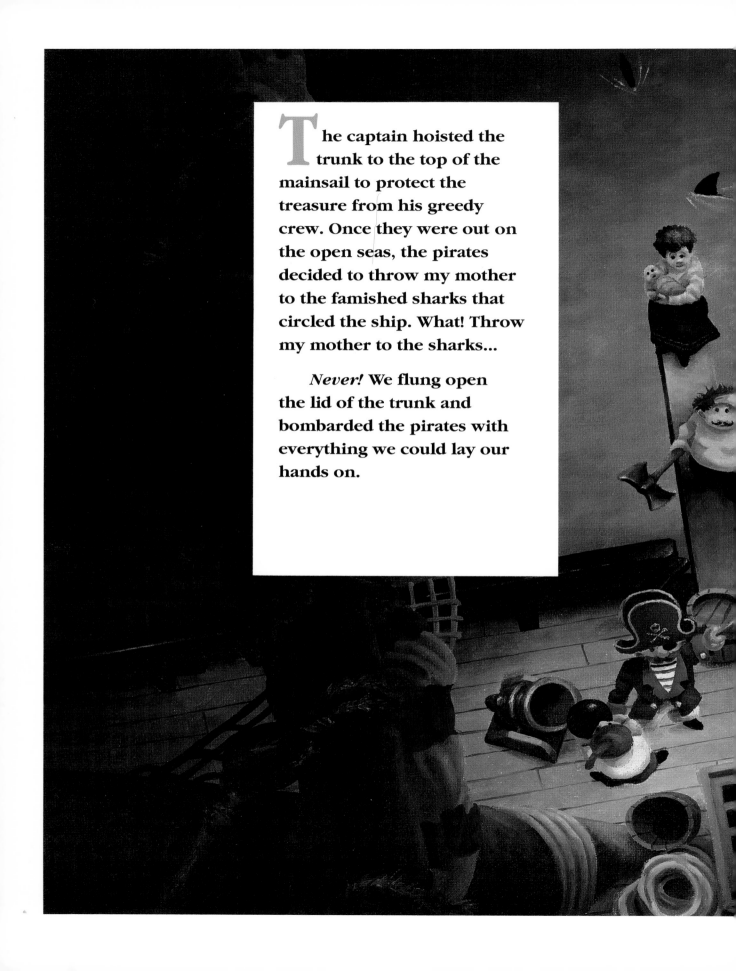

The captain hoisted the trunk to the top of the mainsail to protect the treasure from his greedy crew. Once they were out on the open seas, the pirates decided to throw my mother to the famished sharks that circled the ship. What! Throw my mother to the sharks...

Never! We flung open the lid of the trunk and bombarded the pirates with everything we could lay our hands on.

The captain flew into a rage. "Stop them! Get them! Fire on them!" The men pointed the cannon right at us and fired. The cannon-balls sailed straight up, right past us, then fell straight down. The ship looked like Swiss cheese. In the confusion, mother lowered the trunk into the water and climbed in with us. The pirates jumped into their lifeboats.

We drifted for hours, bounced around by a storm and the huge waves that almost swamped us. Martine spotted a ship on the horizon. Was this one friendly, or was it another pirate ship?

We decided we couldn't take a chance. We hid in the trunk.

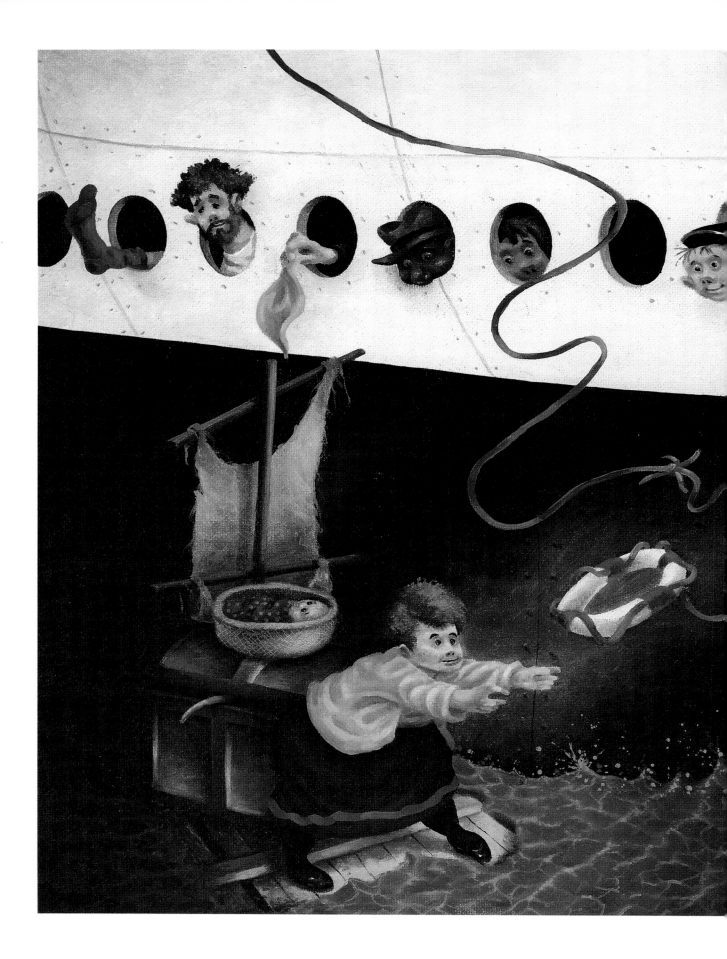

My mother peeked out of the trunk and saw it was a cruise ship. But she was worried that we would stupidly ruin everything once again, so she told us to stay in the trunk.

We agreed. But the dog had to go to the bathroom; then Martine, Normand and Johanne had to go too. Then we all decided to go find mother, just to make sure that the last few days of her magnificent cruise would be carefree and comfortable.

Other books by Stéphane Poulin:

BENJAMIN AND THE PILLOW SAGA
MY MOTHER'S LOVES
Stories and lies from my childhood